Writing 26

The publication of this book was supported by a grant from
the National Endowment for the Arts in Washington, D.C.,
a Federal agency created by an Act of Congress in 1965.

Pamela Millward

MOTHER
A Novel of the Revolution

San Francisco / Four Seasons Foundation

Library of Congress Catalog Card No.: 76-78045
Standard Book No.: 0-87704-015-X

Cover photograph by Steamboat

The Writing Series is edited by Donald Allen and published
by Four Seasons Foundation
Distributed by Book People, 2940 Seventh Street, Berkeley,
California 94710

Part One

**to the Men
who kept us alive**

They were braiding the hair of the maiden. Round and round, layer after layer, it had been parted into the smallest possible divisions which were being separated into further categories and woven into the smallest imaginable braids, each one no bigger than a pencil and most no bigger than the lead. Leah's hair was eternal, a mystic bush of light brown fuzz that flared out from her scalp in a solid pyramid.

As long as it's pouring down outside, we can't worship the sun. The study house leaked, and the tatami mats were soaked. There was an Eygyptian picture to follow, of one of the guardians of the inner tomb of King Tutankhamen, a lifesize child of gold over wood who stood facing the huge closed door, and whose outstretched arms delicately blocked and caressed the entrance. The calm gold face waited devotedly in an attitude of perfect grace and innocence facing the tomb of her king. Paul, I want to get *up*, she was giggling uncontrollably, giggling under the peculiar prickles of restraint a silly million braids caused to her scalp. Not yet, her dark young man replied, as though speaking to Mama's child, who was also standing in the room to hold a handmirror. I want to see how this does. He smiled at his audience. You may never need to do your hair again. At the end of each braid was a tiny loop of colored embroidery silk, which should be tassels, they decided, and Mama's child stripped a godseye for yarn and silk to provide tassels for Leah's adornment.

For all this the hair should be thick, with bangs. The problem is to get the braids to hang down equal lengths without cutting them. He tried looping the longer braids back upon themselves, tying them up with a little twist of silk behind the ear. This gave it the proper fulness. One of the few really stylish hairdos in the world and no one had used it for 4000 years. But those were people of leisure Paul, said Leah, they had nothing to do but keep a good many people around to do it for a specialty. Mama sighed loudly from her

3

book in the corner. She conjured helplessly when it rained and she always conjured people at their worst. She wished it would stop raining soon, so she could go outside and try to stop reflecting. Surely they were all there out of love, indoors.

You look truly beautiful, she whispered of Leah. No, I'm slipping back, was the sad reply, despite these thousand tugs of affection. Mama had met Leah at a yoga demonstration on the grass of Golden Gate Park. Have you ever seen this one, she said, and performed an intricate movement of various positions, with the hands always held *so*, cupping water, cupping air, the breathing deep, ruffling neither air nor water, the eyes downcast and inward, gazing deeply into the reflection. The first time Mama had seen Leah complete this one she said Wow, what is it called. Looking Into the Mirror of Karma, replied Leah, bouncing up again happily. Mama was very moved. It was enough to make one weep to see that pure gaze even now, through the complicated braids, directed in a dance by her lover. It's just an adaptation, she said modestly. The original dance is very ancient. In fact it's lost.

No, I'm slipping back, she said. Yesterday was an entirely adverse day. Yesterday Leah and Paul decided to come to the end of their sexual life together, such bellowings, weeping, declarations to pursue individual paths to spiritual peace and calm, a car screeching to a stop, a spiritual reconciliation, and today it is raining. Separation is the only answer for us, Leah announced, more than once, only then will he be able to achieve unity with the universal moment. Her huge eyes today were radiant with tears.

Perhaps this should be the initiation rite for everyone entering the ashram. The offhand comment hung in the room. Enervated though she was, Mama knew she couldn't sit still for that. She fidgeted again, trying to disconnect her eternal spirit. All my wires lead inward. Mama's child had helped for the first half hour, but her fingers soon got bored and she dropped out of the braiding to hold a mirror. That held her interest and kept her quiet. The absolutely calm blue eyes of her own child gazing back at her. What

do children think about, the pure in heart, and when does the
process start? What shall we do today and what's for snack? We
could always measure hair. Paul, their shortest, had recently grown
out from a shaved head. Perhaps he would want to shave Leah's
head. Would she follow him into red seas of baldness? She was a full
biblical woman, attentive and devoted.

Leah's months under the sun had turned her hair many shades,
marked in several layers of yellow brillo. The lighter strands
appeared and disappeared even through the smallest braids, tiny,
glossy, now no bigger than a line of sesame seeds on new bread.
Soon they would all be as tiny as poppyseeds. Why doesn't the sun
shine in?

There was no spiritual peace that day. Even in the evening Mama
entered the room of sleep as a quarry slave to do the dishes, and
slept in a cold bag. Paul, across the room, wrapped the drapery of
his couch about him and lay down to pleasant dreams. Leah and
Mama, awake, brooded over their spiritual inferiority. This was the
only dry room of their retreat, and the child bedded down by the
fireplace, all the others leaking, leaking. Try for the silent mind,
they whispered for one another, as they said Goodnight. God bless
you, think of me when you undress you, Leah was startled, afraid
Paul might take that wrongly. Nightnight, sleeptight, don't let the
bedbugs bite, continued the merry child.

Paul sat up smiling. I was dreaming of Her, he said, speaking of
his spiritual advisor in India, whose book he would translate as soon
as he had mastered Hindi and Sanskrit. She was saying to me, some
people can't even bring me flowers without them wilting along the
way. O Paul, what a beautiful dream! cried Leah. I was thinking the
same thing, thought Mama, everything I touch turns to shit. She
was going soft in the long rain. Try for the silent mind, they whispered for one another once again, but the flux of Maya swished in
and out of her head, and ran like tears in her ears. Will you shut up?
WILL YOU SHUT UP, she roared in her mind. The fire flared up
in the dark and Leah turned, moved the child over slightly and

tried to make her engorged, braided head comfortable at last on a pillow.

You may never need to do your hair again. Mama worried about everyone from the same damp bag. There was so much dumb energy cheerfully lost from the heads at the ashram, given in irrelevant currents, mingling the wires of the hair and eyes. She mourned a human energy warp, the eternal loss of whom you lay you down by, entangled in hair, wound round and round. You love the first person met in a vacuum, the beams of the moon come down and tangle you, crossing your wires here or anywhere.

If you think that's weird, thought Mama, I met my husband at the junior-senior prom in Erie, Illinois.

In those early days he could dissect her language critically, pointing at any single given word. But what does that word *mean*, he would triumph. Because of course she didn't know, or couldn't say. White man speak with forked tongue, she blazed, I know what it means. Just you wait. You don't know anything, you're just saying *words*, was their favorite remark to each other. I KNOW WHAT IT MEANS, I TELL YOU. I do, she sulked. You shit. You're nothing but a shit. But Jack to her dread in her dreams tearing through a manuscript. A whole catalog of nasty laughs. Once Mama typed a paper for him for a philosophy course and he accused her of inverting a proposition with incorrect punctuation or something. I thought you'd left it out, she said, giggling in embarrassment. He had her hair in his hands. YOU THOUGHT I'D LEFT IT OUT. He used to tell this to their college friends to humiliate her in public but one day he woke up and he really was shorter, and then he got very nasty. Smart guy, eh? he used to say, A Wiseass that's what you are.

The dance was called Holland Polonaise and was preceded by a dinner in the high school cafeteria, and as part of the entertainment, after the reading of the Class Prophecy and the Class Will, a girl in a lilac formal stood up and *whistled* the "Indian Love Call," complete with trills and lotsa vibrato, on a bird whistle she had hidden in her mouth.

This is a dance upon nothing at the end of a twist. Stranded in Oakland some months later, Mama wrote back to friends:

I lay down a lot but I don't sleep much. I guess I'm not being very brave here in Oakland. Everytime I put my head down on the pillow there's old Will with his eyes wide open on the next pillow with his head all wired out and his brains scrambled. He looked so different before he left. I saw his chin and his neck for the first time. I feel so sad and don't know whether to miss him or not. Once in his dealing days he was sitting on a park bench in Marin City with his hairy arms crossed over his chest and the hair pouring out of the neck of his shirt and down his back, hair sticking out all over his head, stoned out of his mind, looking like a grimy but very cheerful hedgehog, and a spade sitting next to him softly and awefully leaned over and asked, What is you?

I guess I'll never know for sure, either.

Mama was well aware that she would take any drug which promised to eliminate the helpless reasoner trapped within her mortal coil. There, always putting it into words again. When the rain let up to fine mist she walked out, going down to the old sheepbarn to see if I can find some more of that dry wood. Let up on me a little, will you. To the child she suggested, you make the tea for snack, ok? Secondgraders can do almost anything. Break my fast with leftover corn bread and camelflower tea. I'd walk a mile for some camelflower tea. A play on words the child might never understand, not sharing the memory of a real radio voice or real radio magic.

She stacked up a few pieces in the sheepbarn for the return trip and walked up to the upper pasture to view the old orchard and the deserted buildings. Coastal November, nothing dies but more white shows. Not snow, but yogic light: white mist cutting up the pines on the opposite ridge, creamy pale lichenflowers weighing and breaking down the apple limbs, silverflowers upon silverflowers, the blight of apple trees covered their broken blanched dead bones, the underbelly of the aspen. This was Mama's first winter in the West, and it seemed surprising that the rain would whiten everything, then produce a second season of lushness which by spring burned brown again.

She assumed a meditation posture in the damp grass, dampening her knees, her ass. There was an old woman who lived in a shoe, she had so many children she could drape her cunt over a stump. She winced at the way sayings still poked at her unawares. There were spots in the redwood grove which were still almost dry, under the heavy huge trees. Leah has given up everything for Paul. Only let me be with you, but she could not give up Paul for anything. Mama rustled in the damp grass, another argument forming in the apex of frowns behind her third eye. Her new friends demanded glory, exultation. How do you determine glory in another person? I am as positive of their religious conviction as a paleface voyageur, voyeur among the esquimoux. Primitive peoples knew what they were doing. They had ritual to back them up. Just because you are USA 20th Century, the intent to worship is as valid, even if there is no ritual here. We must create a new ritual. An ashram is a community for the concentration of spiritual power. Look, I've heard all this before. Let me ingest anything, or any combination of electronic sounds. Trapped within a mortal coil. There, shuffle off, will you? Putting it into terms and counter-terms again.

She wished herself rooted into the wet grass. A famous yogi when meditating believed his hair, grown long, would reach into the earth, and waited for the consciousness of that binding, emanating root. There, on the upper meadow, she could sit forever, watching over the aspirants streaming up the road, the young in hordes, all streaming to the country to talk to the trees and listen to their own hair grow.

They had visitors, but none stayed too long, In the heat of the next summer they expected quite a few to come and dig holes into the earth and live there for awhile. The orchard would bear, the taxes were paid, they were housesitting for a friend. Their visitors frequently left pledges behind, sleeping bags, stereo sets, which they abandoned as they went back to the city for a weekend dance and unexpectedly found themselves on the way to Big Sur, or Denver, or the Taos thing. At this moment a sleeping bag was dripping onto the floor of the study house from a line strung across the room. One of their visitors had left it behind. He was a tall man on his way to Samoa. We're really brothers, he and Mama used to joke, because his hair was the same color and length as hers, except she shaves her beard. That was the sort of remark a child overhearing might remember. When the baby was born it had tufts of vestigial hair, black, three inches long, on the backs of its ears. Kid looks just like Grandad, her fatherlaw had said, haw. The child's hair was now just the right length, since they now believed in the interchangeability of souls, it didn't matter if the kid looked like a girl or a boy, or grandad.

Mama found time to memorize the light of every grove. There were redwood, apple, and the crescent, dappled sadness of eucalyptus. Beneath that stippled light the acrid drippings of the eucalyptus ruin the soil and sap the surrounding trees, yet nothing else produces the quiet flutter of that drooping light. Dragging her toes in the fine ruined soil came a girl, followed by a young man. A girl nibbling her own hair, pale-eyed as a goat, stripping the fine leaves and buds from the trees as she passed. I cannot believe she is truly a nature lover, she touched every living thing she passed, put her hand out to the branches, dragging them slightly after her, stripping the ends off fine leaves and buds, the tips of ferns. Little leaves fell through her fingers in a constant spray as they walked along, the young man following, almost drawn along, and when she shook hands one noticed a slight green grass stain to her fingers. This was Belinda, who came with Will.

As soon as Leah could find Mama alone she announced excitedly,

Paul thinks Will might be a person of true spiritual power. He shook hands strongly and radiated contentedness. He's the most open person I've ever seen.

Will's amazing eyes pulsed like a cheerful cat. And he said the most fantastic things, like: Cats really know how to meditate. I always figured cats really knew where it was at, he commented one night by the fire. There's not much variation to them and they seem to come and go, die off and merge with the Oversoul and come right back. I think they're too smart to evolve.

He was happily carving something out of wood, following the lines and drilling it, finding faces and shapes. The finest compliment he could give to anything was to stroke his mustache and hmm. The nice thing about it, he said, is that it doesn't look like anything else.

Religious abstinence, eh? Well, it don't seem to hurt your figure none. And the little one's going to be something when she grows up. Your mama's rice bowl, he told the child, will never be empty. He pulsed at Mama. Of course, she said. They never had such a supper in your life, and the little ones chewed on the bones o.

Let's split a trip, she said, sometimes it's very beautiful. They decided on the sea, and went down together.

They looked at a tide book and timed their high with the tide. Should we be up when it's in or when it's out. If we go when it's out there's more space and we might see some weird things uncovered. Do people clam there, Mama asked. Clammed out. We get off near the amusement park. We might see some weird things uncovered.

Mama wanted to leave the child at home. She worried because she wanted to. Where are you going? the child asked, why can't I go too. On a trip, on a trip, they laughed. Stay here with Nick and Little Nick. You're going to the beach, the child accused, and got a pail and shovel. Be good, they said. Seriously, I'll bring you something back. From the belly of the whale.

Take a good look at everything. It's going to be an important day, they believed. I can tell, the sun is shining. It was going to be a day of great conclusions and summations, resolution, and above all, change. Take a good look at me, she thought to the child, it's all going to be different when I come back. They sat round the table one more time with Nick and Little Nick, and drank a mix from saki cups. The children had 7-Up for breakfast.

It was a good thing Zee was planning this, because everything was on time, timed before hand, timed with the streetcar, tide and sunflow and that was the last time there was time.

The streetcar down the avenues clangs at every corner, turns, turns, pulls up a grade and down straight towards the sea. Through the front windows of the car, past backs of passengers the tracks of the streetcar aimed them gleaming for the sea, visible in the opening between buildings at the end of the line. Terrible slow and terrible funny. They stumbled off at the turnaround and began to walk through a glass-strewn underpass (grass-strewn underpants!) under the great ocean highway. Halfway through the glass changed to sand and they ran through diamonds to the blazing sea.

How nice, how nice, Mama thought, plodding, placing her feet one before the other carefully, deeply, in the sand. What I supply she lacks, what she fills I need. Especially the feet. How fortunate she wore boots! Tossed my shoes in the sea, immediate, as soon as my feet flew up. And now we make a pair, she said, cheerfully, to no one. It was the first time in her life Mama was content to be inane.

The city. The city has so many angles and textures, patching and jutting, the complexities blur and dull us. What she actually said was, Lines so dull. The sea is simple, sand to water, sticks and glare, bulbous weeds that walk up onto the shore and twine around your legs. The waves became slow and iridescent. As they rose up, blocks and pyramids that were pushed up from the depths, hexagons and polyhedrons, pile and topple, the sea life peered out, suspended, keeping their motion inside huge tears of ice, clear grey, that fell down, foamed. All that happened in the space that Zee said, The sea, look at it in a those, in an interested long voice, and then began to cry. The sea. Past the surf and the mist it was level, endless. You never shut up, do you. O Lord, have mercy, Thy sea is so great and my ship is so small—that was a Norwegian fisherman's prayer, with appropriate typeface under a black and white picture of the sea, an old man and a child in a boat, now where did I see that? O for chrissakes, in the Sunday Supplement of the Chicago Daily Tribune a million years ago. You never shut up, do you.

They squatted behind a bush and peed like little girls. A young poet on the boardwalk pointed out their familiar glitter to his friend, who was a newspaper man visiting from St. Louis. He was very moved by it. The bodily grace of dope. You see, he exclaimed to his friend, the newspaper man, this is the first time in history people have had the means to try to consciously change and illumine their lives.

We make a pair. I am bovine, placid, mute, she chatters beside me of Nick and Little Nick, so vivacious, quick and small. I am strong, aryan, dull, she is slight, dark, syrian. They held hands. She remembered gathering milkweed in Illinois under a blazing sun, walking down a hot railroad track. Two kids in town shoes running a three-legged race for the war effort. We were supposed to drag it back in a gunnysack to the grammar school, to be used for lifebelt filling.

They held hands. Sailors couldn't talk to them, Give us a kiss, honey, they hollered down from the railing, swinging their blue belled legs down over the sea wall. No thanks, no thanks, I've given up fucking people I don't like.

A little girl puts sand in a beer can and whirls around, playing shakey shakey shakey in the sun, her own fine mist rising and falling. The children in the glare of the surfmist at the line of the sea are all the same size, the same indeterminate color of skin and suits, dark grey upon a glaring haze.

When I first came to California I came out here at night and the top of the boardwalk was covered with fog. I could make out the boardwalk pilings and thought they were people standing up to their hips in water, facing the ocean. Intently watching beyond the ocean. I thought they were fishing or something.

And what if somebody *is* watching? There are lotsa people watching. All those little surfer girls just waiting, carefully baked out on their towels, for someone to discover them, to justify the outlay of big money on boards, this year's swimsuit, bodycreme, hairbleach, a line of cars facing the ocean bucking under her vision, twisting and bucking, barely restrained to their parking lots.

The high set in like a tide, and she must needs sit down, stunned by a terrific burst of agape, frightened and apprehensive at the breakdown of heterosexual possession, yet smiling stunned at Zee and at the ocean, hearing her insides speak of learning to love correctly.

They decided on the sea, and went down together. Look it won't break, honest. I'll show you, it never breaks. Down the hall the sound of water, Jack's whoop, Look at this, look at this, she approached cautiously down the hallway to the can, hey, look you silly girl, at this, he was laughing and shaking, taking away from the water-faucet a balloon, huge and long and white as his leg, as thick, and bounding, vibrating up and down, shimmering, bouncing it like a ball from his hand, laughing so hard she shrieked as the huge scumbag broke and splashed all over them, what is it, what *is* it, that huge against his leg, shivered and slopped water all over the bathroom.

Promise me you'll always test it, she whispered. So we'll know if it had a leak. Get up now and test it. So for the first two years of their marriage he got up into the cold with the limp skin in his hand and went into the bathroom. There he threw the condom down the toilet, turned on the warm water, flushed the toilet, took a washcloth and carefully washed his penis and his legs, went back to her and gave her a hug in bed, see, it was perfectly safe, he said. By the time he got back to the room his organ was unpleasantly small, cool and clammy.

She had lost her bag of milkweed silk. She couldn't find Zee for the moment, and her jaw began to ache from the widest of all possible laughters.

A young poet on the seawall pointed through the crowd and further explained to his friend, And at a lightshow dance, no one touches, but everybody MOVES. 627 boys and 594 girls, none of them dancing with a partner. The young are interchangeable! His friend took notes.

She couldn't find anyone in the haze, but nothing of them doth fade. Nothing of him that doth fade/ but doth suffer a sea change? into something/ ?Rich and Strange. Nothing of him that doth die/ But doth suffer a sea change/ into something/ rich and strange. There was the sound of a fire snapping nearby, a blaze crackled on the sand. She perceived that the sand was drying out under the fire. She perceived that the water sorted and smoothed with each hand all the possible alterations. She perceived the alterations.

She was crying because his head, which had been struck by a shovel, when his body was unearthed, his head fell back and split in the flames, she was crying because his smoke was greasy. Promise me the man is great enough that only his body is burning, his heart will be retrieved. She crawled forth like the land-sea-otter-man from an unwelcome mythology, an apparition no one was happy to see. Why are you burning, she asked the man behind the fire, the man in the fire. To get at the heart of the matter, he said. The port authorities insist that this sort of thing may not be buried, but be first destroyed by fire.

She was distracted from the body of the bather. Perhaps she didn't have the heart to continue this story. His heart was pulled from the fire and presented to his wife in an engraved box as a memento. Lord Byron swam out to sea to look at the blaze. His greasy smoke. Died at sea. Died at sea. If the soul hurls out to sea in

a glorious arc and a lame poet swims after it, and if that moment
had always struck her as the single most poetic moment she had
ever read about, and if he swims after it, it's nothing, I used to swim
the Hellespont every night before snack. Your body is burning.
Nothing is ever going to be the same again. Nothing of him doth
die/ but suffers a sea change. These words were written on stone.
She was distracted from the body of the bather, terribly distracted.
Back to her field, which was English Literature. I AM TRYING TO
KILL THE OLD WORLD, WILL YOU SHUT UP????? Break.
Break. Break. On thy cold. Grey stones. O sea. O for chrissakes,
she'd lost it, sail on, Dupree, Sail on sail on.

Nick took the children down to Foster's for a bun and his morning coffee. They sat each with their own tray and their own bun and
their own glass of water, and refilled the glasses of water. He
showed the children how to open one end of the paper on their
straws and shoot the papers at one another.
You can't take a woman or a kid. They always want to know
where it's going to End Up. He understood the courtly deference of
the hillbilly, next in line, to the misshapen rabbitgirl of his dreams.
She goes out of her head when she fucks, bright green orlon sweat-
er, grey pleated skirt, pleats satout and billowing around her, much
too long. Her elderly parents, or an aunt and uncle, in eyeglasses,
scarves. Are we all of the same family, at every table? The hillbilly,
lean, army fatigue pants with pockets on the legsides, he too understood: You can't take a woman or a kid. With a woman or a kid you
can't end up puking in the men's room at the Greyhound Bus
Terminal, or asleep on the ground at the Rattlesnake Hilton outside
Albuquerque. Yet the lean young man fished down into his legsides
for yet another sweet for his darlin'.
Mama wants a brand new man, but she's too old. She thinks the
problem is the kid. Beautiful kid. But who wants a kid. The young
have their babies under trees in Golden Gate Park, believing their
screaming will be eased by the bird of the Baby Jesus. I leave him

with my mother, said the little surfergirl. A baby at 16, I mean,
Jeez, I want to get out a little. I was married once, she said, for
about a year. Long as it takes to have a baby. But my old man
wanted to go to collich, and I knew it wouldn't work. The young are
so much more rational these days. They can always tell at what
point it won't work. Send money, Papa, I want to get loose. Nick,
rabbinical, redbeard, turned his blazing blue eyes on a young man
with a little bareass girl in a pretty dress riding upon his shoulder.
Her blonde hair hung down in sausage curls. His hat had a broad
brim and a sweeping feather, like a cavalier. Casually across his
back she had one fair tiny hand against the collar of his blue denim
jacket, little maryjanes hung down by his hip. Looking around at
everything light as a feather, like the bear and the dandelion child,
and the bear caught fish for everybody.

   Nick assayed the women passing by, the waitresses with garish
linen fluffed above their bosom pocket like a huge handkerchief
rose, fastened forever with the name of Fosters, yowling casually
Singul Muffinnn! over the counter, assayed also the women on
Geary Street, and decided he would much rather live on Potrero
Hill than any other district in San Francisco. The most beautiful
women in the world lived on Potrero Hill, fatassed bowling queens,
for example. There was nothing to the Berkeley Look, which all
depended from the shoulder bag, from the pocketbook. The girls
may look very well-fed from the rear, beautiful hair, but they're
always frowning, just getting used to their contact lenses, hurrying,
with their possessions slung from the shoulderbag, one hand resting
on the bag or gripping the strap like a man opining, with his thumb
stuck in his suspender.

   The most beautiful women in San Francisco, maybe in the whole
world, lived on Potrero Hill. A line of trees bent over the play-
ground mothers with their babies, long grass flattened by wind and
lovers, the hill sloping down to the freeway papers blowing against
the wheels of the baby carriages. Irish-Armenians, Japanese-Jews.
He remembered Ruth and Omi, their father used Nick as a

connection and had to settle down to a lab technician's job because the old lady, Japanese old lady he had too, had run off and left him with the kids. Omi, at four, This icebox is *filthy!* cleaning out the tinfoil wrappers and the mescalin. Puerto Rican teenagers in diamond hose and minitents so short the bottom row of lace on their panty girdles showed when they raised an icecream stick to their lips, but the bowling team! Curly-headed short-waisted blondes, showing nice gluts in blue slax, children in the grimy streets, Tibetan liondogs, small nasty little dogs tied outside Chinese grocery stores. Fong said, don't tell me yr troubles, just pay me dollar money. And how he yearned to snap her bra, the way she might dodge, yet pull her arms back, the elastic band showing like a bar of whiter white under her white sport-collared T-shirt.

Zee was successfully recreational, and successfully unemployed. He knew Mama's admiration for Zee's pure scent, which was musk and grass, sperm and the strong oils she rubbed on her gleaming face and body. There were plenty of women like Mama still on the bus, still working at the lowest and least competitive of jobs, twentyfive and thirty and supporting an old man, barelegged and runlegged in cheap flat shoes and a very plain coat, long dun hair held back with a leather or wooden circle, the hair parted in the middle or pulled straight back and absolutely uncut to reveal the unmade face, tired perhaps, wan, but believing the compromise reduced to the smallest possible margin, where Fong mumbled, don't pay me your troubles, just tell me the dollar money.

Mama's child asked, What's a cyclops? A cyclops is a giant with only one eye. Are they ever children? I don't know, cyclops have children, I suppose. Will told me there was a child all locked up, a beautiful child, who had one eye. The third eye. I think I have a lump on my head. I think I have a headache. Ouhr! Monnstr! said Little Nick. Monnstrs was his favorite game. Growlings and Ruhrrings over the breakfast bun. Once I showed them the stars from

Sutro Garden. That's the big bear over there, where, are there really bears here? No silly, on the sky, the outline of a bear, over there above the water. The children kept looking behind them for bears. Once the patterns of the sky are pointed out to you they are unchangeable, can always be found, but until then all the points are the same. Shadow man. Nick moved his family to the desert, which was cold and hot and very clean, and Little Nick sent back a picture of the pawprints in the sky, configurations of pure animal tracks, the stars as he saw them.

Ruth as a child just big enough to baby-sit, answering the phone, Oh, Nick, just a minute, I'm holding Little Nick, let me put him down so's we can talk in private. And Sasha in the cold cold house, skating across the waxed floors, playing ISPY with the children in the empty San Francisco flat, Victorian, using the glass knob on the French doors as a spyglass. ISPY he cried, Doorknob! Joy wells up, the beautiful, in inane endless rhythms, the same melodic line over and over, the words are interchangeable, Who's gonna shoe your pretty little foot? Who's gonna glove your hand? Who will take your picture when I'm gone? I will, cried the hippie, not even noticing he had stepped into Nick's eyes, but photographed nonetheless, photographed in the blazing blue eyes, the outlines, I will never forget you.

And they beat Mama and Zee back to the flat by hours and waited for them to come crashing unsteadily down the hall, laughing and shushing and gripping the doorknob mysteriously. Mama burst in singing, still intently listening and amazed at the angelic chorus flushing up and down each arm, till she got fully into the room.

You've been working day and night! she screeched at her child, who was intently holding up a picture for her notice. I can't take all this! The disorder spread out before her in a vast mess, covering each room, scraps of paper, paste, crayons, she grasped at the child's arm in a futile adult gesture, lipstick and paint gooed all over, **Oh God**, she groaned to the child, I thought you'd look different.

Part Two

In Illinois the child was always sick. The cold of the winter and the pollen of the summer were blamed. Every season had its curse.

The wooden floors of the farmhouse were cold. They were bare, except in the parlor, which was unused. One day in January after Jack had driven slowly away from the snowpiled house, she decided to polish them. She showed the child what she was doing. They had their sweaters on. Turned the heat up as far as it would go, turned the oven on and swung down the oven door in the kitchen, and crawled around the house on their hands and knees, scrubbing the wax on with rags. This is the way we clean our house, wax our floors, clean our house. She ventured into the crisp cellar and got a brick for the child, wrapped it in a flannel rag. Now iron the floor, make it shine. She herself used a contraption found in the closet, an original Johnson's floorwaxer. Broomstick handle swiveled onto a fivepound square of iron about two inches thick, wrapped in a heavy felting. Use like a shuffleboard stick. Apply wax, leave on twenty minutes, go in next room, come back, floors are glossy but not wet, rub to a high shine with polishing apparatus.

She sang a song to her child to the tune of "You Are My Sunshine": You are my polishing apparatus, my lit-tle polshing ap-a-ra-tus, you make me hap-py, when floors are grey, Mama's songs always had more syllables than notes, somehow the tune gets lengthened. The child, in her socks, skated and glided across the dining room floor, laughing and coughing. The house reeked of floorwax, a sharp petroleum penetration. We'll have to open the doors and let all the cold in. You always end up trying to heat the whole outdoors.

When the father came home the child was still sick. Pease get well by the time the car turns up the road. You know how he is. Coughing, red eyes, runny nose. It's either a cold or an allergy. My poor little girl, he said, what did you do to her? Has she been outside in the fresh air today at all? By the time they ate each night it was dark. Their conversations and the damp had already caused the dining room wallpaper to part from the wall and droop down in long, dismal, tears.

The father and the mother slept upstairs in an unfinished second floor. Better not sleep up there in the wintertime, the real estate agent said. Cold enough to freeze your vaseline. The child was downstairs in her room, and between them the sides of the stairwell were rough unpainted plaster, bitterly cool but not clammy. I always say the difference is the wet cold, it just seems like it's a wet cold where you are, and it just goes right through you. Here we have a dry cold and it just don't seem as bitter. Her fingertips grated down and up the sides of the stairwell, scraping on the roughness, barely touching, as she made her trips to check on the sick child. I can't breathe, mommy. Can I come upstairs and sleep with you. I don't want to walk, it's cold. My feet are cold.

Her coughing woke him. You've got to do something for that cough of hers. I have, I've been up with her. Did you try the Vicks. I tried the Vicks. She needs an aspirin. I gave her some. You've got to make her sweat to break the fever. Go make some tea. She won't drink tea. Go to sleep, let's go to sleep. It's warm here under the covers. I can't breathe. Well, she's choking to death, that's all. The child was moaning, wanting only to be held. She wrapped it in a blanket and sat on the edge of the bed, rocking it back and forth. He sat up and glared at her. Do you realize the oxygen is being cut off from her brain? If it doesn't get in her lungs it can't get to her head. Why don't you do something for her? I'm rocking her. He threw back the covers and went for more aspirin. She's already had ten grains, just half an hour ago, I don't think she should have more. It can't hurt her. Take this for daddy. It might be the allergy. What did you do today, did you do anything different? The whole downstairs stinks. What is that smell? Please, we waxed the floors. What's in floorwax, anyway, go get the can and see what's on the label.

It's the smell that's doing it. You'll have to get rid of that smell. You'll have to wash off all the wax. It wasn't possible, of course, and they had to stay up there and shut the door and live in the cold. The only way to wash oak floors without ruining the finish, as a matter of fact, is with elbow grease and kerosene.

In her fondest dreams Jack would find her sitting on a park bench. She would be wearing, beneath her hair, a pinstripe suit with crawford shoulders and lapels and a miniskirt, white crocheted stockings, and handmade archepedic oxfords of pierced blue suede. All from St. Vincent de Paul, pray for us: he expected to find the mugged nude corpses of a British male midget, a nurse and a little old lady buried under the nearby rhododendron bushes. Better go away, would be her chance to say it, inhaling deeply. Even the water fixtures around here say split split split, they crossed a walk and a cold arc of water came around from a sprinkler and splashed her ass. Who says dinner must be on the table when papa comes home from work? Is there ever joy in Mudville? Who needs the Bicycle Irish?

Jack could read the passages on head while drinking beer in his car, drunk for the ignorance of her yeasty mustiness, an overflow that clung to her skirts like an oldlady smell. He never knew for sure whether he liked it or not. Definitely not when they were going to a party. Old ladies were always overperfumed. Clean on the outside, dirty on the inside, the German side of the family bible used to say, running whitegloved fingertips over a windowsill, but never quite breaking in. Is that remark supposed to pertain to me? the Irish side of the family bible shouted.

One of the passages was: Putting the temporal in its proper relationship means the renunciation of the attraction of hasslement, prying away the ego-hold of the will-I, won't-I, won't-I, shilly-shally, plans of the future and anguish over the past. Oral lovemaking is the ultimate in nonattachment. Love which does not demand its own orgasm, as the acting party foregoes coming to concentrate on the orgasm of the passive party.

I always tell my girls, when I show them how to wash, that sure there's an odor (either the medical term or the color or some exclamation of the nurse was "weeping lochre"), but you don't (said the nurse, hoisting the legs of the patient) have to smell like you have a dead rat stuffed up inside you.

Mounds of soft white muscleless flesh. She lay on her back, her stomach was down around one side, she could see her toes again. The nurse piled it all up on top. Symmetrical for an instant. It slipped away to the other side. The nurse piled it up again and sank her fist into it. No sensation. Sank her palm into it, rubbed and punched. You've got to find that lump and rub until you bring it up to a hard ball inside. Nursing will keep it hard, helps the uterus contract. Mama, closing her eyes, thought she'd said, keeps the universe intact.

Mama kept a journal about everything. This one was entitled TANTRAUM—A Dream of Love.

Mama was watching them make love and she didn't like it. She wondered if he were watching too. His face looked mad, locked out. He had closed her eyes but she could still see their selves and hear their music. She was hearing the noise and making the noise, destroyed and detatched, engrossed and so watchful. She was sure he was out of his head and across the room as well. You just don't care about me, she sighed.

Beneath the stunning level of his energy they were creating something, but she couldn't imagine what. Considering everything (but what was it that was doing the considering? everything on the bed was lost), what was watching ticked off all that had been done, she was sure he hadn't come, had done this, moved to that, and there, a touch of the mouth moved them to take another turn. Not talking at all, nonverbal weight and pressure (ouch!), she considered he hadn't come yet, and found herself turning, falling and moving

*under him, and they did that too and she came again. She came
seven times and found it unlucky (this last was underlined in the
margin with the chortle* NOT A BAD TITLE IF YOU PUT IT IN
CAPS. *Mama really liked long titles).*

*Finally they just quit, stunned. Had either of them said
anything? The objects of the room came back out of the dark, more
of them each time they breathed: the end of the bed, a velvet hanging, the dresser by the window, and on the dresser her bracelets,
heavy-leaved plants, cigarette papers, a plastic baggie full of dope.*

*He sure could make her unhappy. She puzzled over his sperm
but couldn't find a way to tactfully*

*(try again) Sperm splashes many ways, well, she knew that, had
felt it against various mucal membranes, seen it wink on the sheet
an instant before sinking into the bedclothes, but she had really
never felt it stay inside a man this way.*

*Shut up awhile, he said, stop manifesting yourself. What? Let's
try silence. Let's try vajroli mudhra. Is it like vaseline? But, Dok-
tor, will it save our relationship? Will it make me a better person?
Will a better sex life make us into better people?*

*What do we do? Just put it in and leave it there. A long time ago,
in the back row of a mysterious Cage concert, she had seen it hap-
pen. Four minutes and twenty seconds of silence and the pianist
doesn't move. The audience is forced back onto itself, to the true
realization of silence. And if there ain't nothin' in you to listen to,
that's what you hear. OK, let's try silences. I'm not afraid of anything new, even if it's evil.*

*Just put it in and leave it there. There's something to do with the
breathing, your left breath goes into my right. Rearrangements.
Continence is the most effective aphrodisiac, because then when
you roll, you roll. Wheel in a wheel they lay, way up in the middle
of the air.*

*What you will hear, he had said, is the ego disappearing. What
she wanted to hear was the tenderness, and breathed deeply, steadi-*

ly, glottily. You're supposed to keep me hard, he complained. She put down an awkward hand between their legs, but he put her aside. I'll do it. I don't want to lose vital fluid. Well, shy or stubborn sperm, where are you? Will we meet at last?

After twenty-five or thirty minutes, cosmic orgasm, he said, in the voice of a countdown. While he was down there with his hand she tried to meditate, he was breathing in her nose and she was getting short in the chest but began to feel her hair grown long, when idly, where he was down there with his hand, he came upon a gummy glot in her short hairs, rolled it between a finger and a thumb, and yanked it out. What you will hear is the ego disappearing, and that hurt.

(try again) Plugged in, she heard their cellular bodies become molecular, and carefully beyond that some ear detected the molecular bodies become electronic, all vibration. If I've told you once I've told you a thousand times music is the perfect microcosm for meditation as it is all vibration and can be created and reproduced electronically. She listened to herself isolate, to himself isolate, saw to the end of it, gave it all up, heard the sperm splashing around in his head, where it would stay, locked forever.

He broke off. Just like that, their relationship became a relationship, he suggested she see other men and was himself seen with a blonde.

His music, which she continued to love, unfolded like a bolt of cloth, as it unwrapped it became wider, a number of stripes were added whose vertical relationships, as in a moving spectrograph, continued at different rates. The music was complex, intellectual, without human voice.

He was seen again at a concert of his works, glowing with cocaine. The program notes remarked: the people of the future, one foot in, as we are, will not appear to have "conscience" in the archaic sense, because they will not be suffering the endless harangue of the unsatisfied inner voice which is futilely trying to rearrange events that are past in time, wishing and excusing it to come different this time.

That's perfect! Leah cried, when this part was read to her. That's exactly what Paul says. Do you realize that after acid the initial obligatory lovers' confession is archaic. The catalog of What Broke Your Heart, what Great Hurt brought the two of you together, who have been the previous painful and unsatisfactory partners. I don't *care* who you are, that's what Paul tells me. The rearrangement of the past in each new alignment is a classic romanticism. Its hope is a waste, because it still puts part of the burden on the partner.

Hear, hear, said Paul. No lovers' confession, no lovers' confusion.

Mama's annoyance was deafening.

(try again) Looking at the Kama Sutra pix: Look at them now, the lordly and individuate, separate, content. They could be fucking anybody. Walls and rooms of smiling faces, full lips, slightly parted, glazed brimmed eyes. A statue is all being and no will, perception and no action, a state of being going into another millennium and not about to stop. The quality is the interchangeability of souls, which occurs only in balance and satiety. Satisfaction on continuum, no rage, jealousy, force, enough for everyone, no babies in this picture, some midgets, no cries or worries, no one has to get up for work at an early hour   (wrong tack)

(try again) Four days in bed with a new lover and mystic spaces separate each joint, disembodied dali-spaces between shoulders, elbows, wrists. Extreme bodily sensations separate the mind from the limbs, a cellular memory of ultimate, nonpassionate warmth. Cut me and I function, Aquarius pours the pure air of reason through me veins.

Will and Mama were discussing whether great spiritual powers were obtained by refraining from sex and dope.

You sure talk a lot of trash for a chick, he said.

Mama was hurt, but one thing pleased her. It was the first time since she came West that anyone had called her a chick.

Will believed he had destroyed his old ego in a drug experience and was consciously building a new one. The first thing he ever said to her when they were alone was, Did you ever die? Hundreds of times, said Mama excitedly. Can't you keep your mind quiet and just sit still without manifesting yourself. All those people shouting inside you, scrambling to get out.

In the mornings she would find him like a huge turnip outlined in his sleeping bag, with only his wooly head sticking out, tapering from his massive shoulders to his toes crossed over, one foot on top of the other. I'm going to stay here until I can know why I don't want to get up, he said, why I have never wanted to get up in my whole life. I don't think I've ever wanted to get up, and I remember wandering around the streets of Fargo wondering for as far back as I can remember, wondering why it was all wrong, everything, always all wrong. And feeling so sad. He wiped his eyes, uprooting the turnip line slightly.

But why pick on me, Mama asked him, you don't seem to want to take care of us. You're too young for a family. WELL, WHEN I KNOW WHAT A FAMILY IS ALL ABOUT THEN I'LL KNOW WHETHER I WANT ONE, he yelled, Will did. WHY DO YOU ALWAYS HAVE TO KNOW MORE THAN I DO? WHY CAN'T YOU JUST SHUT UP AND LET ME FIND MY ESSENCE. You could tell he was a powerful man. It was always leaking out of his eyes and the top of his head and his cock. I WANT TO KNOW WHERE IT'S AT. I WANT TO KNOW WHAT I'M ALL ABOUT. I know I have a lot of power, he calmed down, trembling, his thighs still hopping like toads in his pants, they do that when he blows his guitar or sits next to a girl. But I have to find out how to use it. Only when I lose my ego, when I consciously die, will I be able to achieve all that my consciousness offers.

He couldn't outtalk Mama in that respect. He was the first person she felt she could really talk to since she came to California, and they were full of all the terms of subjective and objective long and short term goals, the alignment of the Kundalini, the gross body and the subtle body, all those people scrambling around inside one.

As for her child, the child never forgot Will's story of the California cyclops, a child attended in an institution because he had one eye, right in the center of his forehead, surrounded by the finest of medical attention but never allowed to be a part of the rest of the world.

It's too frightening! The third eye! They can't handle it! What a beautiful sight that child must be, mused Will.

I'm a bear, see? and you scoop out the hole, like this. It's your job to do the cooking, and you do it this way, you scoop out the hole and you line it with this skin, right? And then you pour water in it, right? And then you line it with a lot of these little smooth pebbles, so the whole bottom is covered. And then you put these hot rocks from the fire in it, see? Only you lay them in very carefully, you can use a split green stick for a tong or a stonecarrier, and you lay them in very carefully, and that's how the soup boils. You can even do it in a basket if the basket is woven tight enough. But you've got to line it carefully, see?

We ought to be able to live on the land at least a year, said Belinda. Or until the next rock and roll dance at the Fillmore. Baby I really want to go into the city this week, Super and Leni and Waller St. Sue and Smokey the Bear are back and there's a big dance at the Fillmore.

The trick is to be omnivorous. Have some acorn mush. But I don't like acorn mush. It tastes awful. Look, you wanna be an

Indian? Go to any supermarket and you'll find that even the sim-
plest things cost money. Storing and gathering, pounding. If I catch
you any small animal you must pound it up whole in a mortar,
meeces, squirrels, add some seed, seeds winnowed from grasses,
jimson weed for a high, acorns, buckeye. Dried and blanched cat-
terpiggles and grubs. Honest, that stuff tastes awful. Isn't there any
way to make it better. Acorn species vary, nor is the acorn really
plentiful, may be bitter to oily, and bound to have worms. Shelled,
dried, pounded in a mortar, leached in water and sun-dried ten
times, mixed with water 12 to 1. Makes a mush thinner than ralston
and thicker than soup.

   Night after night they sat before their fires, arguing force vs.
stealth. If we go with a gun or fire, the ranger will want to know
where we are and why. If no gun, you must be omnivorous and
quiet, and live on the small game. Can you catch a fish by diving in
and bringing up a salmon by grabbing him behind the gills? At the
sound of flying birds, quail-chirr is the exact noise, set fire to this
bush, which is fastflaming. The birds will be dazed, hypnotized,
moonlit by the glare, and can be clubbed. Deer are stalked with
reverence, using a decoy, sticks rubbed together to sound like deer
antlers. Pick a slow deer. Pick a very quiet bear.

   She checked the recipe for slugs one more time and read:
Because they are scavengers living primarily on animal feces, slugs
must be kept for several days before using them for food. To allow
them to clean out their digestive tract, keep in a covered container
containing cornmeal or oatmeal, and wet leaves. Change their food
mix at least twice. Slugs can be parched or sun-baked in a covered
container, then diced and used like clams for chowder. The Yellow
Banana slug is an especially large type found after rains or in mar-
shy spots.

   He pushed her hand into the hole, the hide, the water. It was in
Chicago on a gritty bridge in sunlight. There must have been a million scumbags float by while we talked on our lunch-hour, like
opaque white turds, moving slowly along the Chicago River. Mama
was trying to work out a joke that would make Jack do some kind of

scatological calculation of how many man-hours of sex that represented. Jack in a good mood could make some great calculations, like how many man-hours of pee it would take to raise the need for more chlorine in the town swimming pool.

The girls in their sleeveless dresses were trying to decide whether it was hot enough to go backless tomorrow, in a sundress or a dirndl. Their dresses were yellow and pink and striped, opposite the railroad general office building on Jackson Street. They were watching the scumbags, leaning against the stone bridge wall composed of a grainy cement and stone mixed together in a process invented by a famous sculptor, whatisname, who also did that huge fountain in Jackson Park. Addie Slaifer said, well I don't know, it's practically backless, isn't it, I mean it shows everything you've got, meaning a few inches from the armpit into the shoulderblade, her white shoulderblades cutting up the office as her rigid back typed furiously on the boss's correspondence, and shaved legs, shaved armpits. Mama was just seventeen then and just out of high school, working for the summer in the big city. Of course I lied to get the job. Told them I had no intention of going to college. She laughed furiously, making ducking motions with her head to suppress it, afraid she might wet her pants, the sun brilliant, the river moving at the rate of 6 scumbags a minute between bridge pilings. The sculptor's name is Something, there's a Senator married to his daughter, Lorado Taft, also made that Indian down by Oregon, Illinois, You know that statchoo of the Indian, we'll have to drive down there some Sunday and take a look at it, it's all lit up at night. And the fountain in Jackson Park is an enormous panorama of crawling scrabbling humanity traversing one wall, a frieze you'd call it, facing across the pond this huge shrouded figure of Time. The whole works is cast in some kind of cement but he put too much sand in and it's melting away, little bits each year, the larger pebbles stick out in glops, the sand and the definition have washed away and the inscription on the back of Time is: Time goes, you say, ah no, Time stays, we go.

Mama has told that story at least a hunnert times, and this time it's told to calm herself, keep her from laughing, ducking her head and twisting her long legs by the huge cast cement lamppost, trying to divert attention from the possibility that she is likely to pee in her pants. There were great raconteurs in those days who told their stories over and over again to produce a mellifluous and appropriate catch in the throat. It was a technique Mama had learned from her own mother, who every Sunday to Mama's despair read aloud Claudia Cassidy's column in the Chicago Sunday *Tribune*, of faraway operas and magnificently sensitive pianists, and geniuses that only Claudia Cassidy could appreciate but she would try to share the experience with you. There were great raconteurs in those days, irrelevant speeches talked about what hit most, what had the most emotional impact in the hot flat dirty sun on the Chicago River. Mama's themes came up like garbage from a dredge, irrationally, but no more irrational than the great racketeers who were found shot on every streetcorner to a Chicago kid, shot everyday in the stories that every kid knew, on his way to mass at St. Peter's, when he walked past the flower shop and heard again how someone walked in with a machinegun and even though there were eight witnesses in there buying flowers nobody saw the guy or his machinegun and they all said they saw the body afterwards but they were just buying flowers at the time.

Just passin' through. Some of the stories were obligatory feelers, the sort of a thing you mention to a person early in your first conversation, because his reaction shows you ever after and for all time whether he is worth bothering about again. The greatest compliment Jack could give to her was to bring someone new home and say, Tell him about your great-uncle who walked out the door and never came back, and it had to be told in just the same way each time, with the postcard right at the end, although no one knew for sure whether the postcard had much to do with it, but anyway he'd gotten a postcard from New Orleans the week before saying simply IT ISN'T THERE ANYMORE ON THE CORNER OF ST. LOUIS AND BOURBON STREETS. And if he says, What's that for, or yeah, I guess that is a pretty funny postcard, but how do you know it had to do with him walking out? Wasn't he really mad at your great-aunt or something? Was anything wrong? then you could scratch him off and feel ok about it.

Just like that, their finest stories were violent and faraway. Jack's best was of a Texas railroadman who said his grandaddy used to hunt coyotes with dogs, killed em for sport, and one time chased a coyote up into this cave where lived the biggest rattlesnake anyone had ever seen. The coyote stood at the entrance to the cave, luring the dogs up, and the rattler bit them. He was so big that the first five dogs he bit died instantly and the next six died before they got them home. The man could remember being wakened in the dark to help bring the dogs into the kitchen, those that were lucky enough to get bit after the rattler had spent some of his venom on the others, and had survived long enough to be brought home. Each place where they had been bitten was swollen horribly, and one dog's paw was as big around as the spittoon. The old venomous snake stood off all the dogs for the coyote, a pair of wild things standing at the entrance of the cave, luring and killing off everything that approached.

Even if Jack was still telling that story well, it was someone else's story he was still telling on the bridge in Chicago, and Mama remembered that day, when they had gotten to Lorado Taft's Indian Chief, something reminded Jack of this old Hudson's Bay trick of boiling water in a bag for tea. The heavy bag was listed as part of the Hudson's Bay kit, and Jack read paper bag for bag and spent a long time figuring out how to do it afterwards, with an elaborate apparatus set up above the stove, with a paper bag full of water suspended over a pot of boiling water, something like a long-distance double boiler, but he never did figure out how to get the water to reach the boiling point while keeping the bag below burning temperature.

To the myth of their youth in Illinois was added the dream of the summer job at $80 a day. Zouvas the Greek came and told them

about it one day at the swimming pool, that there were jobs with
the highway department working on the new interstate highway
through Chicago. The outer city was surrounded by cemeteries,
which had made the acquisition of the land difficult and had
delayed the highway for several years. The right-of-way was
secured by tracing the relatives of the remains in the plots and getting written permission to disinter and move the remains. It meant
tracing some families for a hundred years since the burial. Your job
is to dig em up, put em all in special shipments and send em off to
be reburied somewhere else. All right you guys, we want this stretch
of road by September. The only hitch was that you had to stay in a
sort of special barracks, like a youth corps, and you wore special
clothes like firefighters, thick white clothes like asbestos suits or
something, and you had to pass through a decontamination cham-
ber on your way off work back to the barracks. But the pay came to
a whole year's tuition plus maybe a car to drive around school,
because they're payin' $10 an hour, and that's $80 a day, and that's
take-home because they pay for your food and lodging.

Somehow the job never materialized, could never be tracked
down, but when all the bodies had been moved over, a lot of people
used the road.

They stopped at a stoplight late at night when the lights forgot to
change. It was a very hot night in July at the deserted intersection
in the center of the still small town. Eleven o'clock, Mama used to
say, guess I'll roll my sidewalks up and go to bed. Rolled her sidewalks up and her bedroll down and went to town. The merchants
allow themselves one big holiday and sale in July and at the same
time try out the Christmas decorations for the next year to see
which ones they prefer, the red plastic bells or the white Rudolphs.
Strings of colored lights and fake plastic greens spread across the
main street in loops before them down the block, and produced a
real longing for snow in the empty streets. Above the vacant

intersection, where only their car waited, nighthawks swooped through the hot night to feed on the moths beating against the falsely tinseled light.

Mama and Will walked out against the fog with a Coleman lantern, listening, their shadows thrown against the fog and reflected back upon them with a motion and life of their own. Who are all those people? mused Will, holding up the lantern against them and listening to the steady drip of the redwood grove in the fog.

The moistening fluid of the eyeball contains minute ripples which may be seen when one looks at a pure surface such as white snow, a clean sheet, or a cloudless sky. The film of the eye is then projected as a greyish or black tangled thread which jerks and flows with the movement of the eyeball. If the eyeball is absolutely still, staring, intent, this string of interference between the observer and the observed can create a hypnotic effect almost impossible to break. When the Eskimos are fishing it sometimes happens that a man alone in a kayak will become hypnotized against the snow and be enveloped in terror, feeling that the water and the snow are slowly rising over him, unless his hunting mate paddles toward him and breaks the spell by reaching over to him with an oar. Such a man usually becomes useless for hunting afterwards and is considered to have lost his nerve. Mama had often watched this effect on the sky, and once observed it through the eyelids on a particularly brilliant blue day. She was on her back in the field in the corpse posture, and had steadied her head and eyes and tried, as best she could, to quiet the flow. The thread beneath her eyelids began to curl, she found her self watching it, and watched it curl upwards like a bit of oily smoke from her self, and she got a take of her body instantly charred and useless on the parched ground.

I heard this sound and gotta great take on my body, ticks dropping like seconds onto the spongey floor of the redwood grove, a tick swimming through flesh, footsteps kicking closer, a little puff of dust and dried loam with each step.

Part Three

Mama got up from bed one day, pulled on her long black boots and said, I'm running away from home.

No you're not, the child said, Who would babysit me?

No I'm not, Mama agreed. But maybe I'll get a job. The child had spent the better part of the last two hours, the earliest and best hours of the morning, playing around Mama's head, watering the plants on the windowsill, watering the plants on the floor.

You don't need a babysitter. I'm just going for milk and cigarettes. She thrust her arms into her daily bag. Go see Eve if you want.

When Mama returned from the futile orderly task of fondling the want ads over a cup of coffee she was twice as ugly. Go see Eve if you want. But Eve was not quite Zee, who had gone to the desert, or Belinda, who had also split the ashram. She was beginning to mourn for her friends, to wish that everything really was interchangeable, and she lit the incense which hung down in a spiral from the old light fixture in the living room, dropping curls of silent ash onto the bed beneath it.

Her hand on the doorknob of Eve's flat, which was not quite Zee's flat, there were the same bracelets over each doorknob (O Mama kept the rubber bands on hers!) O incense burning in a littered house with the window wide open and the old untrimmed roses on the alley fence getting flatter and looser each year, growing wild, beads and necklaces and bits of cut glass stringing down the knobs and drawpulls on the dresser, Benares silk scarf blowing from the window. All of Zee's life seemed to be painted in that room, painting her eyes, on the bed with the babies, rubbing noses with animals of every temperament, laying her syrian nose to nuzzle everything. Leaning out of the bed in the morning in her Japanese wrapper the children would bring her a marking pentel and she would draw on them. Tattoo me, the child said, holding out her

41

long thin bare foot to Zee propped up on one elbow, the sun shone on the stylized chyrsanthemums of the kimono, Tattoo me, and there appeared a lizard on each foot, tail to toe, wiggling up the upper, spread across the instep, the scent of flowers blowing across the room past the faded Benares.

In Carbondale, Illinois, where her motherlaw lived: Well, she's divorced, you know, and she lives in California. That gave everyone a map for Mama, it meant an apartment in San Francisco, sunglasses, a view of the bay, a job in the Financial District, an Oriental bachelor to take her to dinner. Career Girl map, Divorcee map. If only I knew what you were doing, dear, she wrote, so I knew what to tell my friends. If she says colored stockings it must mean color coordinated tights, the California-sleeveless-turtleneck-shift-and-matching-hose-look that all the cropped-hair lady lawyers wore. Bronzed, sunmottled arms, a largebanded watch with thin gold numbers. Please don't send me the Deserted Woman map, or the Grass Widow map, or the Back Street Wife map. I've always wanted my girls to have a Career Girl Look. At the exact moment her motherlaw wrote that, which was hidden in a letter asking Mama to please list their sizes and colors for Christmas, Mama was introducing her graceful child, the motherlaw's grandchild, to a tall powerful woman met on some wandering, who kissed their hands in greeting, pressing them in her long hands soft but firm, her hair wisped back in a loose knot, triplefocal smokey eyeglasses, strong slim body in Marlene Dietrich slax, a famous junkiechick so perfectly preserved in morphine that there was for her, no map at all.

I wanted the cash, thought Mama. I've lived my entire life in this entire USA and never found anything designed for my personal use. None of it fits, it's either too early or too late. She was dismayed at the gift from Illinois that she had just opened. Her relatives had spent good money on a Spiegels charge account, for a twopiece black rayon laminated suit with a full black fox collar. She would

have to begin an elaborate trading ring to turn the suit into as much
cash as she needed to buy unbleached muslin and old lace table-
clothes at St. Vincent's, to rip them up for chasubles to sell at the
Renaissance Pleasure Fair. First the suit would go to a resale shop
on consignment. When the money came through from that, she and
the money would go to St. Vincent's, there to check the bins for lace
and look for any other saleable clothes. An old suit with an I Magnin
label could bring almost as much as the new black fox. Mama made
lists of journeys, lists of things to buy as soon as she had the money,
but chose instead to stay inside the house and listen to the radio,
keeping up in her own mind the thrilling complexities of ragarock
and folk radio, keeping her own commentary on the times as infi-
nite as the numeric progressions to be found in baseball scores. Just
yesterday she had been struck by the shimmering voice cutbacks
and overlay tracks in the Beatles' "Yesterday." How do they do
that? He's timeless, can't be breathing, they've cut off the normal
fraction of a second it would take to inhale a quick breath, he can't
be getting any older, either.

Mama lived in that place, two large Victorian rooms on Buchan-
an, leading into one another via french doors and polished floors,
completely bare, not bohemian bare, not covered with hip posters
and madras hangings, but just completely bare. There are two
symmetrically arranged mattresses, one in each room, and a salmon
box which doubled as a toybox or a typing table, depending on
which of them was stronger on any given day. From which Mama
looked out onto the scene. Slowly we are building up our material
strength by filching boxes from the orientals, wooden boxes, barrels, red-incised soy inscriptions on blackened barrels. She looked
out on four young men from the Japanese community in weird
clothing, one with cowboy hat and long mustache who looked like
six parts of the magnificent seven and one part Tenzig Norkay. He
loves those little hippie chicks, sees two little mothers walking down

the street, soft dresses blowing back against their bellies, blackhose, hey commere commere, he teases them about opium and howlin wolf.

No I certainly am not living with a man, she said again to Miss Everdike. Miss Everdike, her enemy, had come for her that day in the guise of her social worker. We have reason to believe you have misrepresented yourself to us, the trim woman said. We have reason to believe you have falsified your income. We will deduct your check accordingly, or we will cut you off, for receiving aid from a man. I never, believe me, have received anything but trouble from a man. You rented this place as a married woman and were living with a man then. Which old man was that? Well, you know how these Chinese landlords are, said Mama, if they think you're single and defenseless they never will fix anything. I just had my cousin come over a couple of times to yell at the landlord about no hot water. Look, I can show you the rent receipt. The rent was paid by money order and I was the purchaser of it. They waved proof at one another, stacks of receipts, notices of demand for payment, requests for statement of budget, cancelled checks, confidential verifications of employment, money order stubs. It's true the phone was in the name of E. Stanyan Pinkerton, not because that's a real name, but because I couldn't possibly get a phone in my own name because I ran up such a big bill last time. I've already spoken to the landlord, said Miss Everdike, and I found exactly what I expected. If he gives you money and he is working we will find out about it. If you find one that's working and gives money I hope you let me know, thought Mama. You must not move around so much. You have moved around a great deal in the last year, from San Francisco to the country, to Oakland, and now back here in San Francisco. Do you have any plans? There's no reason why a person. When Jesus enters our lives, Miss Everdike, said Mama, distinctly, our choice is no longer our own. There was the beginning of a duet, which began Surely you, but Mama's voice won, quite distinctly, Surely you cannot criticise me for moving around so much when I tell you I am following the dictates of my religion? Surely the state has no interest in my religion, Miss Everdike. I am trusting in Jesus and I'll be sure to find a job real soon. It was a punch that Nick had taught her, long ago when they had first discussed the possibility of her going on Welfare, and it closed the interview.

That time they got out just in time. You could see the outline of their bodies on the sheet, outlined in smoke stain where the smoke had crept up around them as they slept.

Did you hear the Golden Horde? Did you catch that metaphor about the Golden Horde coursing through the body? He didn't wait for Mama's reply, but went on to consider the analogy, It's really quite apt, you know, I suppose it derives from some kind of genetic memory, a recapitulation sensation in the cell released by the drug experience, don't you think? My mouth felt this morning like the Russian Army had walked through in their stocking feet, Mama offered, but it wasn't what the young man wanted. He wanted to listen to the Golden Horde, and had gone with the others to hear a poet read of it, and now they were talking, crowded into a cafe, a whole table of professional graduate students in tweeds and their faces turned occasionally to the small grey woman who sat at one side of the table, conversing with couriers, receiving messages from other tables, representatives of the younger academic scene in Berkeley, the Sexual Freedom League, the League of Eastern Wayfarers (who sold hashish fudge door-to-door), the Kamikaze Press, the Afro Students League. The small grey woman had come from the ghetto of New York to visit their brightly-lit scene, and they found each other of enormous mutual attraction. Mama noted them eyeing the woman with feigned casualness, almost overhearing what she was saying. They were not quite positive that there was nothing in the woman's poetry, nothing in her presence. It was not simply luck that had brought her from the ghetto to the University at Berkeley, it was not simply perversity that extolled

drugs and revolution, and it was, from the size of the audience at
the reading, popular. She was now discussing the establishment of a
new university, she seemed to know everyone, and surely she had
the energy, as evidenced by the fact that she had simply stayed
alive and continued to publish an excellent revolutionary mimeo in
the middle of the worst possible starvation conditions of New York
City, her friends dropping off like flies from addictions to various
despairs, and she had lived to tell the tale. She could not be dis-
missed. In fact, she refused to acknowledge practically everyone at
the table. She and Mama, when introduced, talked about their children, slightly, just a few questions, Mama was the one questioned.
She didn't want her child here. The grey lady was speaking now of
her Free University, where all could come to study and raise their
own food, which would attract all the great old irregulars as teach-
ers. The grey lady's consort mentioned a few powerful and astound-
ing names, the names of men who had been associated with the
finest experimental schools years before. They had offered her their
contacts, they were at her disposal. Casually the young men fin-
gered their steins of draft; had they heard correctly? Surely it was
dim in the cafe, the consort did not have an aura of dun streaked
with filthy black. It was everyone's imagination forming an Armag-
gedon, and if only they knew for sure which side provided the white
horses, should we ride out now? One thing was for Sure: the Free
University was Hers. Her consort clinched their uncertainties by
reminding them that there was this beautiful-love-free-Indian feeling that was sweeping America, and he mentioned two names that
he was sure would love to be in on that, and one name of great
astonishment, because he was now teaching in a large Eastern
university, and that name himself, *whether he knew it or not*, was
going to drop out in a few years, and when he did drop out, it
wouldn't be back to the Southwest, because he *wouldn't be able to
help himself*, that was *the way it happened*.

Thousands blocked the intersection. Out of all those marching, it
was Mama's luck to spot Renata, and be acknowledged by her,

cautiously at first, they had perhaps hoped that they really didn't know each other. But it was indeed Renata walking along behind the huge banner and photographs of the burned children, and Mama, although she had originally only wanted to cross the intersection, fell in and walked along.

They were trying to place each other, get up-to-date. You're not in that religious place, that ashram, any longer, are you? Spend all my time on the bed in Oakland, thinking. Mama was hoping she wouldn't place it, couldn't quite remember herself, had she actually sent the letter to Renata?

Mama remembered that in the course of writing the letter she had become so excited, feeling that she had again stumbled on something which at last unified all her conflicting thoughts and emotions, so excited at the *feeling* of expressing everything she was *thinking*, that she had not only sent one copy of the letter immediately to Belinda, for the ashram library, but had scrawled another envelope for a copy to Renata.

The letter insisted on coming back, page by page, with the leaflets and the posters, as they marched along. HELL NO— NOBODY GOES! hung in the air above and before her, beside the first page of her memory: *Dear Belinda—Away from the ashram for a few days and visiting friends on the mesa. Taping commentaries on the good news of the Revolution we talked and taped for hours last night about two new books we both value, we talked our way to our own view of the necessity of looking at the core of the thing straight on and unflinchingly.* (She went on.) *This morning went to see some neighbors, Renata and Steven S., who lost their eldest daughter (10) this week in a horse back accident, the horse stumbled in a chuckhole and the child fell, just off balance, just the wrong angle, not far nor fast and was killed instantly. Renata is a tall woman of great presence, dominant nose and eyes, short-cropped mahogany colored hair, fair skin, long arms and fingers. She has four other children, a goat, a cluttered house many-*kindered (Mama had particularly savored that word! It seemed such a fortunate choice!) *with kids' paintings, toys, kodacolor snapshots, socks, lots of breakfast dishes in the sink. A small house with a lot of additions and unexpected turns. Steven is a carpenter and has built new rooms with each child and now has a skeleton of brand new house on their property (raw yellow wood in the mist—Bolinas mesa is all brush and mist in the morning). I wish you could have been with me because I am sure that the colors I saw this morning had the key to the total tragedy, to acceptance of it and the placement of death I am trying for in telling you this. If you have seen the colors we could be silent! She in her morning robe of chartreuse coming to greet us in the mist, a bit of aqua ribbon threaded through the lace. (You know that friend of ours with the dog, she irked me so when she extolled her dog, she lauds that dog for behaving like a dog, over a second huge stillborn, and going right on to the next pup, as an example of spiritual power, silent mind and true Bhakti Yoga!) She talked to us of the memorial service, they are having a memorial service for the neighbors on the mesa, her hands were making bouquets of flowers which were to be placed all over the house, red and yellow African daisies, white tall spikey flowers, bright blue delphinium, purple lupines, all field flowers her children had gathered, had spent the day before roving all over the mesa gathering as many flowers as they could find. She said her youngest, practically a toddler, had brought her two sunflowers, enormous heads he must have asked a neighbor for, as they are at least four feet over his head. She talked of the composer's Prayer for Children, which he will play tonight, which he wrote when Nick's nephew (10) was busted for grass, the investigation of the home led to threats to take the children away, so they brought Roman back from the Village, he shaved off his little beard and went back to school, this time to public school, and is perhaps relieved to be not living with his father in the Village, as there was nothing much to do there, you can't really help your father be a poet, except talk junk to his junk friends. Just a matter of simple time, the kid is only 14, so out of that came the Prayer for Children and the Welfare got their mother a job as a clerk in a Jewish cemetery and insisted that she keep it. No more money, we taught you to type, now you support yourself.* (And the dog wagged his tail, and looked wonderfully sad. O All we wanted was to be one step beyond Cool People!) *Back to the colors—the house has an imitation tarpaper-brick-printed face and is full of surprise nooks because of the add-ons. The interior is mostly wood, the lighting hangs from the ceiling with the flypaper, bulbs on cords shaded by baskets, chinese lanterns in the form of paper fish and smiling crepe paper suns and moons. Renata has trimmed all the flowers down and tied them in bouquets, has used all the vases and jars and coffeecans and has given us a bouquet of oranged daisies and two stalks of white foxglove. She picks up a heap of greens, stalks and leaves, and we walk outside to give them to the goat. We are saying our goodbyes, she shows us where they will plant a willow tree, the white goat rises to his knees from the bed of yellow straw and accepts the gift. We are standing in the mist, grey road, the goat accepts the flower RED, all of Renata in a bright robe, we hear the footsteps of another neighbor on the road, she appears from the mist going to the morning mailbox in her bathrobe and pajamas, bleached blond hair in curlers, that bathrobe is bright PINK appearing against the high grey broom of the dirt road, we keep saying our goodbyes, the colorful pillars greet each other in the mist. Belinda dear—I found this sequence truly comforting. Love, Mama.*

I CAN HOLD NEITHER HAWK NOR DOVE IN MY HAND said the familiar child with the bandaged stump of arm. Oh, do something! Do something! Renata continued to keep her pace calmly in the thousands walking through the streets. That's a pretty blouse, Mama commented, wishing to say instead, I regret having uttered a letter I may have sent you. This was my wedding blouse, said Renata, smoothing the beautiful white and black Mexican full-sleeved blouse, the kind with pull stitch embroidery and a multitude of tiny black silk thread tassels, Steven and I ran away to

Mexico to get married. She gestured to the crowd before her. Will you go to the end? No, said Mama, I've already gone too far.

　　She approached Mrs. Jackson's head, which was peculiarly waved. The back portion of the hair was perhaps shaven, or clipped to a fine quarter inch of fuzz, while the sides and top were marcelled in fine tight finger-waves that met in a ridge at the top of her head. Mama wanted to touch her head, it had the look of a phrenology chart, it was perhaps infinitely soft, infinitely shiny. It was difficult to distinguish the lines of the hair against the absolute blue-black of Mrs. Jackson's skin. The children were climbing in and out of the shattered window, which Alma the landlady wouldn't fix. I wanted to give you the television, so your child could have some ricriation. She just loves the teevee when she comes over here. I can find you a job and the end of your troubles, because I'm a worker, a worker for the Lord. I got us a new one, and that old teevee was busted, but my little Joe, he can fix *any* teevee. I want you to use this grocery cart to get your laundry back and forth. There was something about the black fine head that Mama couldn't touch. There was something that made her odd, too, a slight sideways twist to her walk and a swallow to her talk, a touch of rickets perhaps, or mild polio as a child. I told him I had the door open for him, leave the door open for him ivry night, just waitin for him to walk in, but he won't admit what he done. He just can't say anything about it. And my worker, she took the girl and put her in another home right after the baby died. It was the shape of her head Mama wanted most, proud and disgusted, angry with Mama. I don't take no gifts back. You've used it, now you're through with it, but I don't work that way, she said angrily. But we're moving now, right now, my friend's car is all packed, and there just isn't room for the television. The children were running in and out, climbing in and out of the gaping window, ducking their heads down away from the broken edge hanging from the top. Mama's new old man honked

the horn again, then got out of his car and poked his beard into the
kitchen. We should leave right now. The room was very hot, summer but the gas heater turned up so you could clearly see the row of
blue flame, the gas oven on, Mrs. Jackson with her slim blue-black
hands on the small of her back, her proud head lost behind lines of
baby diapers covering the kitchen on lines strung back and forth.
The floor had just been mopped, and all the chairs were stacked on
top of the table, so that the entire kitchen had been squeezed
upwards towards the damp warm ceiling, which left the bottom two
thirds of the room completely bare and just the right height for the
children to walk around, although their mother, her head and
shoulders disappearing behind the diapers, hollered and shooed
them off the clean floor. Mama couldn't believe it. She couldn't
believe the endless routine that went to keep the house clean, she
couldn't believe the baby's name was Lazarus. The two small
little boy-spades lugged the TV back down the stairs. The next
one I get's going to be a color teevee. I couldn't afford no color teevee this time, but the next one's going to be color. But I don't
want possessions, said Mama helplessly, and I like sleeping on the
floor. I've always slept on the floor. If necessary I say it's good for
my back. The chile should have a bed. When I was packing, I found
some dresses for your girls, and a blouse for you, I'm sorry I didn't
have the time to iron it. But I do not want a television, I have separated myself from that world, and I don't want to vote, and I don't
want to enter any of those contests where you pay $1 for the puzzles
and if you win you pay $1 for a set of harder puzzles and if you win
you pay $5 for a set of the hardest puzzles and if you solve all those
you get a lottery chance on $10,000. I don't save soap coupons or
enter contests, I don't help people who do. It's ricriation for your
chile, they all need it, said Mrs. Jackson. Why what's gotten into
me, I completely forgot to get your new address, was she being
sarcastic? blue-black sarcasm in her gentle sideways voice in the
humid room. Look, you keep it here for me, Mama said hurriedly,
and I'll come back for it when I can. I'll just be storing it with you,

but it'll really be mine. I want you to know it's yours, Mrs. Jackson said emphatically, I don't take no things back. I want you to know I gave it to you.

Mama figured a bathtub would work for a sensory deprivation tank, if you were quiet enough. It was an experiment in turning everything off, the lights, the street outside, the shades drawn, but she dripped a lot getting in and out and making adjustments, rugs under the cracks in the door and wet towels soaking up sound on the bathroom floor.

The right temperature and the right angle to insert her flesh between the layers of porcelain water, and slowly and quietly laying back, the warm water evenly closed each ear. It wasn't the same as the picture diagram. She was still breathing. So she did that for a while, regular and glottal as possible, and the displaced water trembled, rose and fell.

The sun set and the water got grayer. She had to pee. I'm not going to look at you, you yellow towel! She laid a yellow banner in the water. Name and form are the processes of illusion. St. Teresa asks us to eliminate the *understander*. She could concentrate on nothing only for short periods of time, then exploded into thought. Clank! clank! Someone in the driveway outside was fixing a car, fucking around, dropping his parts repeatedly on the cement. Clank! She roared out of the quiet water, remembering the day when Zee on the street had yelled to someone hanging out of a car hood like a tongue: WHY DON'T YOU STICK YOUR COCK IN THE GROUND WHERE IT WILL GROW! YOU'LL NEVER BE ABLE TO FUCK YOUR CAR NO MATTER HOW HARD YOU TRY! Clank! Clank! I just want to be able to get it into the garage, lady, before it rains.

The water wasn't holding still or warm enough. I'm not strong enough for this life. I will not look at you, you yellow towel. When you ran the water and were underneath it certainly thundered. Try absolute silence. That makes me think of home, somehow. HERE-SMOKEYSMOKEY! COMMÉRE STUPID! The landlady Alma whopped her huge meaty hands against each other in her graveley voice HEARREEDOGGYDOGGYDOGGY waiting on the porch next door for the dog to come barreling, flattened with joy, down the road. Listen Alma, I gotta tell you about this leak I've got. The whole wall of the bedroom leaks. The water comes down inside of the wall, see, and runs along this crack at the baseboard. DOAN-FEELBAD! Alma graveled at her loudest. I just spent a lotta money on this place and mine next door and my whole ceiling came down in the rains. I put a whole new roof on this house. Look, Mama said, the trouble is, see, the roof doesn't extend far enough. It's all new but it's an inch-and-a-half too short and it doesn't feed into the runoff, it just comes right down between the walls. So Mama had drilled three holes in the floor and drew a large orange arrow on the wall with the sign DON'T RENT THIS PLACE UNTIL ALMA FIXES THE LEAKS. IT COMES OUT HERE.

Alma was wrinkled, tough. Mama's skin was getting white and spongey. She didn't want to think of home, of her own mother. HOW'S YOUR HUSBAND? Who? Oh, Will. Oh, well, he isn't here. Went back to Fargo. I always try to look after my girls, Mother said, you know how I worry.

So there might even be two Almas! Momdike and cheerful, tormented and embarrassed! Tormented to tears, they just used terrible language—IT'S A BRUSH FOR YOUR BRUSH!—the ladies' club shrieked themselves to creases about the bridge prize of a bath brush. WE SHOULD HAVE GIVEN HER CURLERS TOO! NOW YOU CAN BRUSH IT AS YOU WASH IT! Her own mother when she came home after ladies' night, everyone half tight with loose tongues, when she told that story gestured vaguely to her sexuality as if it were an infirmity or attached to her leg somewhere near the knee. You know at a bridal shower they have someone take down all the things the bride says when she is opening her packages and then when everyone is a little tight from the spiked punch someone reads it back like it was the bridal night dialogue Ooof OOOF what is this thing anyway? How do I unwrap this, I'm all thumbs. Such nice heavy ones, and both the same color too. It's not too small, it just fits. Again? ANOTHER one!

Was there something of that in Alma, too? She was coming up the back steps for the rent 10 days late. Look, can I get you a job, a girl with your training ought not to have any trouble anywhere. He's gone back to Fargo. He wanted to do it his own way. I GUESS THAT'S IMPORTANT FOR A MAN, HONEY, TO MAKE HIS OWN MISTAKES. Now how about getting a nice job with the Ladies' Marine Corps. You could begin as a lieutenant. She heard her transistorized music move hazily up the stairs and stop outside the door. There *must* be two Almas! Alma was a mother, too! The landlady adjusted the chorus of distant voices confined to her box. She couldn't hear any of Mama, but stared at all of her white dripping flesh within the kitchen doorway, Mama flipping a wet towel across the floor with her foot wrapped like a mermaid track, Mama who wanted to say something so full and loving, in recognition of all the facts, I SEE YER BUSY, SWEETIE, I'LL CATCHA LATER, hollered Alma at the door, as she backed down the stairs. But which one would pay the rent?

You've got to choose your animals carefully. It has to be just the right animal at the right time. Otherwise your ark will sink.

They came back to Oakland to find the war economy dominant and unquestioned. High above the drear avenues were posted the first of the government slogans: across a green plain, soldiers ran, firing into a smokey jungle. The sign said BUY US SAVINGS BONDS WHERE YOU WORK. THEY DO. Within 3 days they had exhausted their stake on rent and food and jobhunting, and realized that there was no place he could support them: his age and possibilities were immediate conscription, and no employer would listen. The support of the woman and the child, which made employment necessary within days, had no legal name to hold off the draft. Student deferments were tightening, but school was the only way he could avoid the draft. His parents had often offered to pay for his schooling, now their offer seemed the only way. Trustingly, they forgot that the father controlled their future: he welcomed the son's immediate return, offered him support through graduate school, and refused to transport or support Mama or her child. A telegram arrived with enough funds for one one-way ticket to Fargo.

They spent their last day across the bay in the park, before a bed of forced flowers arrayed in designs. They sat on the grass to the side of the bandstand concourse. The child immediately found playmates in the crowd and left them. The concourse was a large dusty area around several pools and fountains. There were hundreds of broad trimmed trees of exactly the same height. They were not quite ready for leaf, and it was noticeable that the clump of runners, the fingers extending from each fist, had been carefully pruned to the same length.

They sat very quietly. In a way they were exhausted from all their changes, they felt he was dying, that he was being sent to die, and yet she was resentful that he would have the luxury of suffering while being supported by his parents. He looked at her with his marvelous eyes. I'm going to die, he said gladly, because only then can I live. In our next life I will be worthy and able to support you. She was annoyed, she thought he was indulging himself in this pursuit of suffering. They looked away from each other and into the sunny haze of the concourse.

Ah, beautiful, he said happily. I knew they would be here on such a sunny day. Come along, I want you to meet them. He strode up the grassy bank toward a man whose black long worsted hair was held back with a colorful braided band. The young man cradled a girl in his arms who was wearing an undefined garment of a beautiful Indian cloth. This was Sair, who preferred the name of Givey, and her husband Norman. Beyond introductions, no one talked.

They sat quietly, believing they were not manifesting themselves. A lady in a pink plaid pantsuit approached them, as any citizen of Paris or the Village, and asked if she might take their picture. Of course, they smiled, as genuine in their love as the lady was intent on capturing their image, if not their essence. They blessed her as she put them in her box. Although Mama saw, from the camera angle, that the picture was really more of Givey and Norman than of herself and the shaven Will, who was wearing his jobhunting and planeflight clothes. She quickly held up a flower between them.

It was shortly after that, that Will began to laugh and Mama began to cry. He was delighted with his friends and the sunshine, she was annoyed. It ain't, she whispered, it ain't funny. His eyes pulsed as he puzzled over her exact words. What-is-*it*, he chortled, repeated in the same gleeful voice that reminded her of when he had held a flower before her in their religious ceremonies and dangled, Thou-art-that. What-is-*it* that can't be funny? She shook her head, the flower on its stalk.

Later, as they rode the bus back down Haight St., she glanced up to one of the turret windows overlooking the street crowded with colorful people, and she saw a figure laughing, a glorious figure in black covered with feathers and beads. He was shaking with joy, bobbing and weaving, leaning out the window. Their eyes met, and it was as though, through the medium of some powerful drug, his whole being poured into her in a palpable joyful stream.

Yet if she had gotten off the bus and run up two flights of stairs and into that bare room, hung with paisley and swathed with silk, a temperacolor mandala painted onto the storefront window, and the young man, she would find him just as beautiful. He might assure her that she was also beautiful, or he might have forgotten that it was into her that his whole life flowed and illumined in a ray, at that instant. And in a way, Mama reasoned (and there's Mama, reasoning again) it wasn't her, because as she looked, he was doing it again, wherever his eyes rested into focus. Was his Being any less Real because he continued to pour out the window completely and into each and every vessel that passed beneath him? Was it any less Real because it was Miraculous, like the bottomless pitcher of a childhood tale?

This novel was written at Morning Star Ranch, Sebastopol, California, in Oakland, and in San Francisco on McAllister Street, and on Third Avenue, from 1966 to January of 1968. It was submitted to a publisher in November of 1968.